Library of Congress Cataloging-in-Publication Data
Printed in the United States of America

One Green Mesquite Tree

by Gisela Jernigan

Illustrated by E. Wesley Jernigan

Harbinger House, Inc.

Tucson

One green mesquite tree
growing in the sun.
Two cicadas buzzing:
summer has begun!

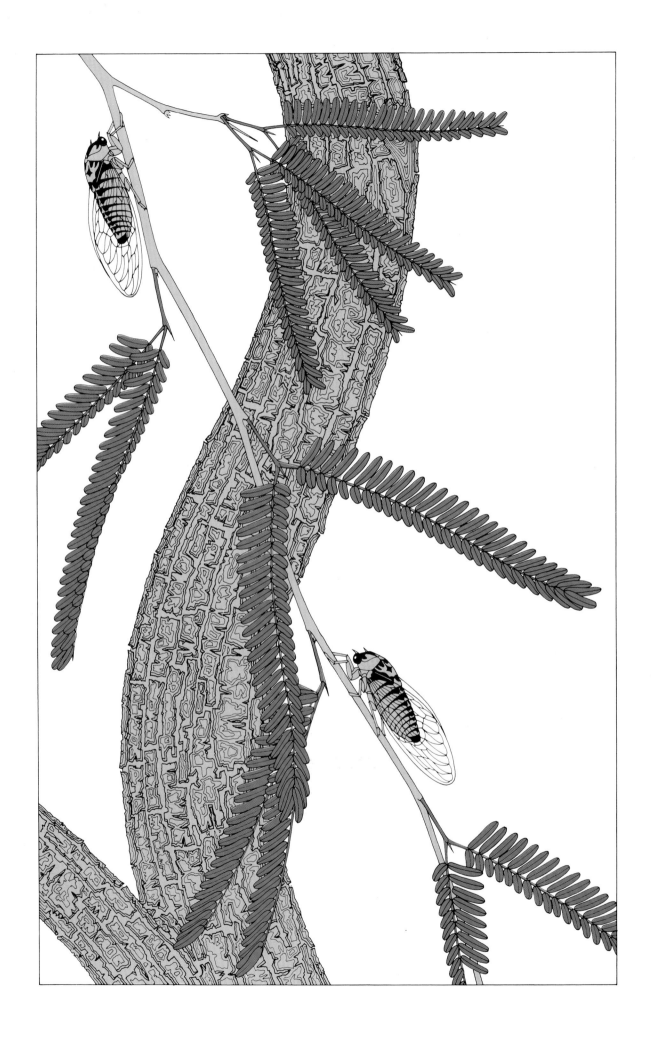

Three tall saguaros
bursting into bloom.
Four purple martins
looking for some room.

Five jumping chollas
needle-sharp with thorns.
Six lively cactus wrens
chuckling in the morn.

Seven palo verdes
form a golden bower.
Eight busy bumblebees
drinking from the flowers.

9

Nine ocotillos
    blossoms flaming red.
Ten emerald hummingbirds
    coming to be fed.

10

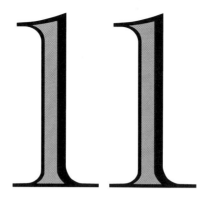

Eleven broad prickly pears
with fruit of flavor sweet.
Twelve desert tortoises
plodding up to eat.

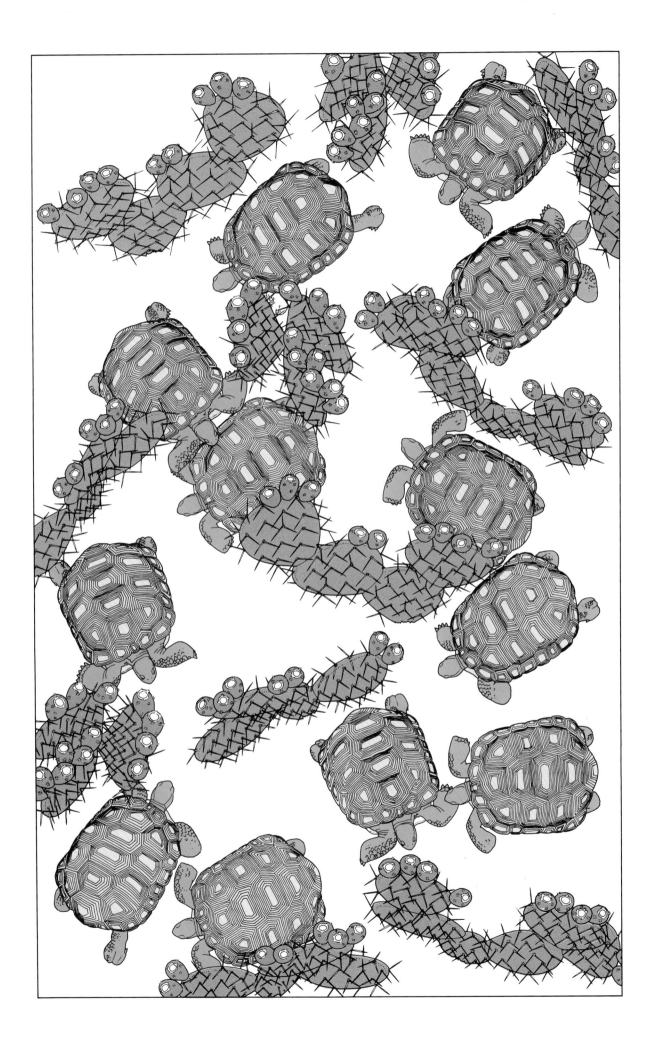

Thirteen fragrant yuccas
with flowers creamy white.
Fourteen yucca moths
come lay their eggs at night.

Fifteen devil's claws,
    seed pods sharp and curved.
Sixteen bighorn sheep
    spread them with their fur.

Seventeen creosotes
    have little water needs.
Eighteen kangaroo rats
    make moisture from their seeds.

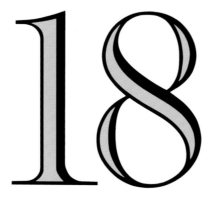

Nineteen barrel cacti
   crowned with fruits of yellow.
Twenty long-nosed bats
   seek them in the shadow.